YOUNG
READERS

Whiteout

BECKY CITRA

ORCA BOOK PUBLISHERS

Library and Archives Canada Cataloguing in Publication

Citra, Becky
Whiteout / written by Becky Citra.

(Orca young readers)
ISBN 978-1-55469-083-1

I. Title. II. Series.

PS8555.I87W45 2009   jC813'.54   C2008-907307-X

First published in the United States, 2009
Library of Congress Control Number: 2008940981

Summary: A near-fatal accident changes Robin's relationship with her cousin.

Orca Book Publishers gratefully acknowledges the support for its publishing programs provided by the following agencies: the Government of Canada through the Book Publishing Industry Development Program and the Canada Council for the Arts, and the Province of British Columbia through the BC Arts Council and the Book Publishing Tax Credit.

Cover artwork by Peter Ferguson

ORCA BOOK PUBLISHERS
PO Box 5626, STN. B
VICTORIA, BC CANADA
V8R 6S4

ORCA BOOK PUBLISHERS
PO Box 468
CUSTER, WA USA
98240-0468

www.orcabook.com
Printed and bound in Canada.
Printed on 100% PCW recycled paper.

12 11 10 09 • 4 3 2 1

To my father, for so many years
of encouragement and support

Chapter One

...Heavy snowfall warning for Vancouver with thirty more centimeters expected tonight...Motorists are urged to stay off the roads unless absolutely necessary... Whiteout conditions...

Robin snapped the radio off. She was totally sick of doom-and-gloom weather reports. She released the drain in the kitchen sink and stared out the window at the frozen lake and the dull gray sky.

If the storm had waited just one more day, her cousin April and her Aunty Liz would already be here. They had planned to leave Vancouver that morning and make the six-hour drive to the ranch by midafternoon.

One more day. The problem with Vancouverites was that they made a big deal out of a bit of snow. They should try living here at Bridge Lake where it snowed all winter long.

Boots stamped on the back porch. Dad stuck his head in the door, letting in a sharp smell of cold and snow. "Time to get the tree!"

"What?" Robin swung around. "We always wait for April. She'll kill us." She forced her voice to stay calm. "Besides, the highway was open again this morning. Aunty Liz said they were going to try."

"It's going to be dark soon," said Dad. He shouted into the living room. "I need my tree-finding elf. Outside. Now."

"I'm coming!" yelled Molly's voice.

With a huge sigh, Robin gave in. She bundled six-year-old Molly into her purple dinosaur snowsuit while Dad went outside to start the snowmobile.

When they were ready, Molly clambered into the caboose behind the snowmobile. Their border collie, Hurly, leaped in beside her, wiggling with joy at being included. Then Robin climbed on the seat behind Dad and wrapped her arms around his puffy down jacket.

Dad headed toward their ranch gate. High snow-drifts lined both sides of the road. It was like being in a long white tunnel. Robin closed her eyes and tipped her face into the sharp air. For a few minutes, she slid away from her disappointment and lost herself in the roar of the snowmobile and the cold.

Just before the gate, Dad slowed the snowmobile to a stop and shut off the engine. The sudden silence settled over them like a soft blanket. Molly and Hurly clambered out of the caboose. They plunged up and down a snowbank, Molly puffing like a train and Hurly barking joyfully. Robin dug her mittens into her pockets and watched.

Dad shook snow off a young spruce tree. "This one?"

Robin shrugged. "Sure. It looks fine."

Dad tilted his head. "Say that again."

"It's fine." Robin hunched her shoulders.

"You've forgotten your lines." Dad raised his eyebrows. "You're supposed to say it's too skinny, fat, tall, short, feeble, scrawny, none of the above or all of the above. You don't say it's fine until we look at every tree on this ranch and then come back to the first one we started with."

"Right," said Robin. "This is the first tree. It's fine."

"Hmmm. What do you think, Mol?"

Molly stopped halfway down the snowbank.

"It's okay," she said.

"Then this is the one," said Dad.

He pulled the cord on his chainsaw. It roared to life and sent Hurly scurrying behind the snowmobile, barking bravely. Dad cut the tree near its base and tied it to the back of the caboose. He brushed needles and snow off his jacket.

At the last minute, Robin decided to walk back to the house. She waited until the roar of the snowmobile had faded before she started trudging along the road, the snow squeaking under her boots. It had snowed again last night, and the gray sky looked heavy with the promise of more to come. It would be dark soon.

If *only* the storm had waited.

Up ahead, a row of Christmas lights twinkled on the barn roof. Christmas Eve! Robin's favorite night of the year. Her dark mood melted away, and she broke into a run. After all, Aunty Liz would have phoned if they'd had to turn back. They were probably bumping over the cattle guard at the highway right now, and Aunty Liz was saying, "Rattle me bones!" like she always did.

Robin raced the rest of the way to the house. She stamped her snowy boots on the mat and went inside. The smell of burnt raisins hit her like a wall. A pot of mincemeat was bubbling over on the stove. Robin turned off the burner. She sucked in her breath.

What was going on? And why was the house so quiet? She peered into the living room. Molly was sprawled on her stomach, coloring a picture of a sleigh full of presents. She was scribbling over the lines with a red crayon. Totally un-Molly.

Robin frowned. "Where are Mom and Dad?"

"They're upstairs talking. Gran phoned while we were out." Molly picked up a green crayon and scratched at the paper covering with her fingernail.

Robin stared at the pile of torn crayon wrappings. "Don't do that, Molly. You're making a mess."

She swallowed an uneasy feeling. She went upstairs and stood in the hallway beside her parents' bedroom door. She could hear their voices, a little bit of Mom and a lot of Dad. Robin knocked. "It's me."

"We'll be out in a minute," said Dad.

And then Mom. "No, Mike. Come in, honey. And get Molly."

Molly was already there, squeezed up against Robin. She raced into the bedroom and scrambled up on the bed beside Mom.

Mom had been crying. Robin saw that right away. A thin icy prickle crawled up her back.

Dad stood up. He kept one hand on Mom's hair. "Gran phoned while we were getting the tree. There's been an accident."

Robin's head filled with a roaring noise. It was suddenly impossible to breathe.

"Whiteout conditions…twenty-car pileup…" The thunder in Robin's head drowned out Dad's words. She pressed her hands against her legs.

"Liz's car slid sideways," Dad was explaining in a steady voice. "A truck hit the driver's side. April has some bruises and cuts, but she's okay." Dad reached down and covered Mom's hand with his own. "Liz has been taken to the hospital, and Gran will phone us back as soon as there's news."

Questions spilled out of Molly. Did Aunty Liz get to ride in an ambulance? Was Gran going to sleep at the hospital too, like Mom did when Molly had pneumonia? Could they still come for Christmas anyway?

Molly didn't get it. Robin pressed her fingernails into the palm of her hand.

Her little sister finally wound down, like a balloon losing air. "Are we still going to have supper and decorate the tree?" Molly asked in a small voice.

"Of course." Dad charged into action. "Come on, Mol. Let's go on a scavenger hunt in the freezer."

Robin stared out the window. From here, the lights on the barn looked like they were suspended in nothingness. Red and green and blue stars.

Last night, on the phone, Aunty Liz had promised. "We'll do our best to get there, sweetie. Our very best."

A sick feeling washed over Robin when she thought of her reply. "You *have* to come, Aunty Liz. *Please, please, please.* I'll never ever forgive you if you don't."

If only she could make those words go away. Maybe then Aunty Liz and April would never have tried to come.

The Christmas lights blurred together, and Robin blinked hard. Behind her, Mom said, "The important thing now is to save Christmas for you and Molly."

The bedroom door closed softly. Robin hugged her arms to her chest, but she couldn't stop shivering.

Chapter Two

Christmas happened and it didn't happen. Dad was on the phone a lot.

"A terrible shock…months of rehabilitation…broken legs…a crushed pelvis…No, the doctors don't know yet…Not the Christmas everyone expected…We're going through the motions anyway."

Going through the motions.

When they opened their presents and Robin saw her new cross-country skis, for a few minutes she managed to forget. Dad stuck a bow on Hurly's collar, which made everyone laugh, and Robin's gray cat, Jellybean, tunneled into the mounds of wrapping paper. The afternoon was harder. Robin and Molly took carrots to the horses, and part of Robin wanted to stay outside forever. Mom cooked the usual turkey dinner, but everyone picked at their food. Molly protested when Mom wrapped the turkey wishbone in a paper towel to dry. "I want to make my wish *now*."

I wish…I wish…I wish…

Robin was glad when the long day came to an end and everyone could stop pretending. On Boxing Day morning, they drove Mom to the airport in Kamloops so she could fly to Vancouver.

Mom filled the two-hour drive with instructions. "Molly needs to get dressed for school before you put the cartoons on. And if she wants a show-and-tell, make sure she gets it the night before. She's too slow in the morning."

School wasn't starting for another week, but of course Mom wouldn't be back by then. She probably wouldn't be home for ages. Robin stared out the truck window. Mom moved on to wearing helmets on the snowmobile. When she got to the emergency casseroles in the freezer, Robin tuned out.

The first week back at school, the weather turned drippy. On Saturday morning, Dad and Molly built a snowman, and Robin tried skiing on the lake. The snow glommed on to her skis in thick wet clumps. Plowing through melted marshmallows would be more fun.

After a canned-soup lunch, Dad got ready for work. He drove a snowplow for the Highways department in the winter. "'Rain, sleet, hail or snow, we must get through,' or something like that," he said cheerfully.

"That's the mailman, Dad." Robin stretched her mind through the afternoon. Five hours of Molly. "Can Kim come over?"

"Okay. Just don't ignore Molly."

Robin got on the phone to her best friend right away. Good. Kim was mega-bored too. A pause, and then Kim announced happily, "Mom says she'll drive me over."

Perfect.

When Kim arrived, Robin said, "Hot chocolate or computer first?"

"Hot chocolate," said Kim.

"Me too," said Molly.

Robin set Molly up in the living room with the DVD of *Shrek* and then fielded questions about Aunty Liz and April while she heated the milk. No, she didn't know if they had to use the Jaws of Life. She didn't think April would be permanently scarred—Dad had said a few scratches. And no one had said anything about amputating Aunty Liz's legs—they were broken.

They had been through all this before. Kim had pestered Robin with questions all week. When Robin pointed that out, Kim protested, "But you never really told me anything. Not any details anyway."

"I told you everything I know," said Robin firmly.

Her chest tightened. Not exactly *everything*. She hadn't told Kim how hard she had begged Aunty Liz to come. Robin carried a steaming mug of hot chocolate with a marshmallow to Molly and then plunked down at the table beside Kim. "What's that?"

Kim had pulled a thick book out of her backpack and was flipping through the pages. "*The Book of Lists*. I got it for Christmas. Listen to this. 'Fifteen people buried two or three times…' Here's a better one: 'Nine unusual mating habits.'"

Robin's mind drifted. Fat wet flakes had started to fall. That meant Dad would be later than usual. It was probably raining right now in Vancouver. Mom had said that the rain all week had washed away most of the freak snowstorm and that she'd had to go to the mall to buy gumboots.

"You're not listening."

"I am."

"'Seven famous people expelled from high school.'" Kim flipped more pages. "Here's a great one. Aaaagh! 'Cutlery craving'!" Kim picked up a spoon and pretended to gag on it.

Robin grinned. "Where does it say that?"

Kim slid the book over the table. "'Really unusual medical conditions.' It's probably better than getting Hula-hoop intestine."

The great thing about Kim was that she never changed. Robin took a sip of hot chocolate.

"Do you want to hear about food and their filth levels?" said Kim.

Robin wiggled her toes in her thick wool socks. Jellybean jumped into her lap and she stroked his back. Her shoulders relaxed. "Sure. Why not?"

"Dad, did you know there is an average of thirteen insect heads in two hundred grams of fig paste?"

Dad swirled water around the sink. "That's it. No more fig paste for me." He wrung out the dishcloth and draped it over the tap. "Molly! Time to call Mom."

Molly always had the first chance with Mom. She told her a long involved story about Sally Penner stealing her chocolate-dipped granola bar from her lunch bag.

Finally it was Robin's turn. Mom sounded exhausted. "Oh honey, I miss you. Gran and I are just about to sit down with a cup of tea. I'll put you on to April."

Robin could hear low voices in the background and then April came on the line. "Hi."

"Hi," said Robin.

"What's up?"

Robin launched into a detailed description of the new computer club at school. "We're getting three new computers and you can sign up for lunch hours…"

April was silent and Robin's voice trailed off. Then April said, "Look, I've got tons of homework tonight."

Robin hadn't thought of April going to school right now. She'd imagined her at the hospital every day. "Me too," she said, relieved. Since the accident, talking on the phone to April was hard. There were too many empty spaces. "I'll talk to you soon."

She sent Gran a big hug. Then she handed the phone to Dad and dragged herself upstairs. Homework. Teeth. Bed.

Robin was finishing her homework when a sleepy-eyed Molly drifted into Robin's bedroom. "I'm waiting for Daddy, but he's taking ages."

Dad was still on the phone? They were going to have a humongous phone bill. Something was up. "Come on," said Robin.

She parked in the middle of the staircase with Molly nestled beside her. Dad's voice was low and steady. "A big decision. Are you sure, Jen? You said before that Liz might be in there for a few months."

Mom was thinking of staying in Vancouver? Robin's head filled with a horrifying vision of *months* of hunting for Molly's show-and-tells.

"Of course, it means uprooting her from school."

Wait a minute. Mom wanted Robin to come too? Robin sucked in her breath as she tested this amazing idea. Then her shoulders collapsed. No way. Dad had said *her*, not *them*. Mom would never leave Molly alone with just Dad. She was too much work.

And then…brain freeze. Mom wanted April to come *here*, to the ranch.

Robin's heart jumped. "April's coming," she whispered to Molly. "That's what they're talking about."

And it wouldn't be for the usual holiday that always sped by so fast. It would be for months. Robin's mind raced with the possibilities.

The girls waylaid Dad on his way upstairs. "Will April get to sleep in my room?" said Molly.

"No, doughhead," said Robin. "She'll share with me."

"Actually," said Dad. "Mom thought the computer room would be best. There's the hide-a-bed in there, and we'll move in that old dresser from the basement. It will give April some privacy."

Molly looked at Robin. Robin shrugged. "Maybe you should let April decide where she wants to sleep."

"Mom did. April said she'd rather have her own room."

"Oh," said Robin.

"I'm going to let her use my *Reader Rabbit*," said Molly. "If she's sleeping in the computer room, she can play with it if she gets lonely."

"Wow," said Robin.

"And *Math Magic*." Molly had a total of two computer games.

"Double wow," said Robin.

Dad frowned at Robin. "Good for you, Mol." He planted a kiss on the top of her head. "And now off to bed, both of you."

Robin jumped up. "I'll make you a bet! April moves into the bottom bunk in my room in three days—max!"

Chapter Three

Robin filled the week with making a *Welcome April* banner. The night before Mom and April were coming, she taped it to the wall above the hide-a-bed. Dad had cleaned up the books and papers that grew in wobbly piles around the room. Molly put Waffles, her second favorite stuffed dog, on top of the dresser.

In the morning, Molly was allowed to miss school and go to the airport with Dad to meet Mom and April. Dad was unbendable with Robin. "Let you miss a socials studies test *and* a math test? Sorry, kiddo."

Usually Robin and Molly rode on a school bus thirteen kilometers to the tiny community of Bridge Lake, which consisted of a general store with a post office, a library and the school. Kids from all the outlying ranches went to school there. This morning, Robin skipped the bus and got a ride from Dad all the way to school. Dad and Molly were going straight on from there to the airport in Kamloops. It was *so unfair*, thought Robin for the hundredth time. She should be allowed to meet April too.

Robin discovered that you could actually see clock hands move if you stared hard enough. School ticked slowly by. Kim got tired of saying, "Earth to Robin," and when it was finally time to go home, she sat in a frosty silence on the school bus. Robin's stop was before Kim's. Kim barely looked up when Robin got off. Robin muttered, "See you tomorrow."

Mom and Molly were waiting in the pickup truck at the end of the two-kilometer road that led to their ranch. Robin climbed in on Molly's side. Mom leaned over Molly and gave Robin a hug and a kiss.

"Missed you," said Mom.

Robin arranged her feet around her backpack. "Me too." She took a big breath. "Where's April?"

"At the house." Mom glanced over Molly's head. "Someone we know has been clinging to her like a crab all afternoon, so I thought I'd give April a little break."

"I have not," said Molly immediately. She bounced on the seat. "April looks almost the same. *Almost* the same."

Robin dug a CD out of the glove compartment. She pushed it into its slot. "Did she grow purple fangs or something?"

"No."

"Three arms?"

"Nooo."

"Orange hair?"

Molly's face turned cautious. "I don't want you to guess anymore. But it's not *just* her hair!"

Molly always backed off when you got warm. Robin turned and watched the snowy trees slide past the window.

Molly switched subjects. "April brought her saxophone. She's going to give me lessons."

"Lucky April." Robin frowned. She hoped Molly wasn't going to be a pest and hang around them all the time.

"And guess what? I get to sleep in the hide-a-bed with her."

"Liar."

"I do too. You can even ask April."

"When?"

"Tonight."

"No," said Mom. She drummed her fingers on the edge of the steering wheel.

"Well, one night anyway," said Molly. "April promised."

"Hmmm." Robin grinned. "She probably doesn't know you turn into an octopus in bed."

"I do not!"

"I better warn her." Robin made a gargling sound. "Strangled in the middle of the night by one of Molly's eight legs."

"Mo-om!" Molly kicked Robin in the shins.

"Owww!" Robin lunged against the door. "I've been octopused!"

"*Stop* it," said Mom. "Both of you. For crying out loud, I just got home. And turn off that music."

Robin ejected the CD. There were a few seconds of heavy silence. Molly burst into tears. Robin waited for Mom to say something, but she didn't. Robin blinked and stared out the window.

What was Mom's problem? *She* was the one who had called Molly a crab. That was just as bad as calling her an octopus.

Mom drove the rest of the way in silence. She parked the truck beside the house, turned off the ignition and rested her arms on the steering wheel. "Sorry." She took a big breath and then leaned across Molly. "Big hug together?"

Mom's hug was long and hard. "I love you, girls."

"Love you too, Mom," mumbled Robin. She opened the door and escaped out her side of the truck.

The old mom—before the accident—had been much easier than the mom who had come back from Vancouver.

"You cut your hair," said Robin.

April was chopping tomatoes by the kitchen sink. She whirled around. Her straight blond hair swung just below her ears in a blunt cut, longer on one side.

Robin couldn't stop staring at April. For as long as she could remember, April had had a thick braid almost to her waist. Ever since grade two, Robin had tried to get her hair to catch up, but it always seemed to get stuck just below her shoulders. But it wasn't just the hair.

It was the small gold stud on the side of April's nose.

Last year, in grade four, Robin had finally been allowed to get her ears pierced. Even the grade *one*s, she had pointed out to Mom and Dad, had pierced ears. But not one person in the whole school had a nose stud.

"I didn't tell!" said Molly. "I'm getting my ears pierced and my nose!"

"I don't think so," said Mom. She picked up a green pepper and stared at it like it was an alien from Mars. "Did you find the beans? There should be a can…"

Dad took the pepper and gently steered Mom toward the door. "Couch in the living room for one hour. Doctor's orders."

Robin had just noticed a pale yellowish bruise along her cousin's jaw. Her stomach did a flip-flop. She looked away quickly. She didn't want April to think she was staring. She poured glasses of milk for herself and Molly. "Your hair looks good, April," she said.

"Stephanie talked her into it," reported Molly. "She lives in the condo next to them. She has her own aquarium in her bedroom like me, but she doesn't have a turtle. She has"—Molly took a big breath and finished in a rush—"tropical sunfish."

"Stephanie moved from Calgary in October," added April. "She's in my class."

"Right," said Robin. "You told me about her before."

April slid the tomatoes into the salad bowl. "She has a crazy family. Four brothers younger than her. And their condo's just a little bit bigger than ours."

Robin thought it sounded awful. She couldn't imagine living with four Mollies. She shifted restlessly.

"April and I took Hurly for a walk," announced Molly.

Molly had probably dragged April everywhere. "Horses?" said Robin.

"April said we had to save that till you got here," said Molly.

"In that case," said Dad, "the chief salad-maker is relieved of her duties. Dinner's early. Five o'clock."

Molly started to drink faster.

"Not you, young lady. I need you to supervise spices in the chili."

Sometimes Dad was useful. Molly had hogged April all day. It was Robin's turn.

Hurly scampered alongside Robin and April as they walked out to the corrals. They leaned over the log fence and watched the horses pick through the piles of hay scattered on the ground. Robin's colt Kedar, born two summers ago, wandered over to the fence for a visit, his hooves crunching in the crisp snow. Robin slipped off her mitten and buried her hand in the thick winter hair on his neck.

"I'm going to start working him in the spring," she said.

"Umm." April's eyes had drifted away. She scooped up a handful of snow and packed it into a snowball. She threw it hard against the barn wall. It stuck for a few seconds and then slid in little clumps to the ground.

"We can do it together," said Robin. "It'd be fun."

"Maybe," said April.

Robin stared at April, surprised. "Why wouldn't you want to?"

"I didn't say I didn't want to. I just don't know how long I'm going to be here. So don't go making a lot of plans."

"I'm not making plans."

April hugged her arms. "I'm freezing. Can we go back now?"

Robin shrugged. "Sure."

The sky had turned velvety purple with a round, almost full, moon. A perfect night to ski on the frozen lake. Robin could try out the new headlamp Mom had brought back from Vancouver.

Robin opened her mouth and then shut it.

April didn't want plans.

Fine.

Instead, Robin concentrated on counting each crunchy footstep on the way back to the house. Three hundred and sixty-four. She could tell Molly. It was the kind of thing she loved to know.

Dad dished up the chili at the stove. It was spicy and mouthwatering. Robin was ravenous.

"None for me, thank you," said April.

Mom was filling a jug with water. "Oh April, with all the excitement of getting home, I forgot."

"It's okay. I'll have a bun and salad. I'm not hungry anyway."

"April has become a vegetarian," explained Mom. Robin intercepted a warning look shot in Dad's direction. Dad closed his mouth and reached for the salad.

"What's that?" said Molly.

"I don't eat meat," said April.

Molly's eyes widened. "None?"

April buttered a bun calmly. "Nope."

"Since when?" Robin's voice came out louder than she meant.

April hesitated for a second. "For a while. Stephanie and I started at the same time. I thought I told you about it."

"I guess I forgot." Robin stirred grated cheese into her steamy chili and watched it melt. She vaguely remembered April saying something about the animal-rights group she and Stephanie had joined. But she was sure she'd never said anything about being a vegetarian.

Probably vegetarians were secretly grossed out when people were eating meat. Robin did a quick survey. Molly had brown juice dripping off her chin. Dad seemed to be taking bigger mouthfuls than usual. Mom was doing the soak-your-bun-in-the-chili thing. Robin had never noticed before how *yucky* chili looked.

After supper, Mom sent a protesting Molly in the direction of the bathtub. "But I was going to help April unpack! I was going to say where to put stuff!"

"Not tonight, young lady."

Good, thought Robin. No Molly to butt into their conversation.

"Robin's smiling," wailed Molly.

"Molly, bathroom now!" Mom's voice had the same sharp edge as in the truck. "And Robin, homework before anything else!"

Robin's grin evaporated. "It's April's first night!"

"And we need to get back into a routine."

What was going on with Mom? Robin sighed loudly. "I'll help you as soon as I'm done, April. I've just got a little bit of math."

A little bit of math turned out to be twenty story problems, Robin's very worst thing. Finally, she stuffed her book into her backpack. The putting-Molly-to-bed noises had stopped a long time ago, and the house was quiet. Mom and Dad were in the living room. Dad was reading the newspaper, and Mom was asleep over a magazine.

The door to the computer room was shut. Robin tried to decide if there was light coming under it.

She squeezed the door handle and eased it open. The room was in half-darkness. Moonlight shone through the window and turned the welcome poster into a long pale ghost.

"April?" whispered Robin.

There was a thud and Jellybean jumped off the bed and stalked out the door. "So that's where you've been hiding," said Robin. She waited a few more seconds and then quietly shut the door.

She carried Jellybean up to her room and crawled into bed. He curled up in a lump under the blankets. "You're a traitor," murmured Robin, scratching his gray head. "But I forgive you...just this once."

Chapter Four

Robin clattered downstairs at quarter to eight. Mom was hunched over a cup of coffee at the kitchen table. Robin poured herself a bowl of Rice Krispies and plunked down beside her. "Where is everyone?"

"Dad's gone to work, Molly's looking for her show-and-tell, and April is asleep."

Asleep? Robin choked on a mouthful of cereal. She stared at Mom.

"She can go to school on Monday. That will give her the weekend to settle in."

"I told everyone she was coming today," protested Robin. "Mr. Nordoff even brought in a desk. He moved some kids around so we can sit together."

"It's April's first day here," said Mom firmly. "She needs a chance to get used to this before starting school."

Get used to what? Robin ate the rest of her cereal in silence. April had spent every Christmas and her summer holidays on the ranch for as long as Robin could remember. Mom and Aunty Liz always said that Robin and April were like sisters.

"Can I take my turtle?" Molly called from the doorway.

"Don't be ridiculous," said Mom. "How do you think you'd manage the aquarium on the school bus?"

Molly stuck out her chin. "You could drive me all the way to school."

"I have a fair number of other things to do around here, young lady!"

Robin winced. Mom didn't need to explode like that. Molly always asked for ridiculous things. It didn't mean that she really thought she would get what she wanted.

She glanced sideways. Mom was staring into space, her coffee forgotten. Maybe Mom had to get used to being home again too. Well, she'd better hurry up.

✳

Robin pushed her half-eaten tuna sandwich to the edge of her desk. She took out a pencil and a piece of paper and scribbled some calculations. It was 12:35 PM, exactly 2 hours and 25 minutes until it was time to go home. That was, let's see, 145 minutes or…Robin sucked the eraser on the end of her pencil and did some quick multiplying…8,700 seconds.

"What do you think, Robin?"

Robin pulled herself back to the conversation. Kim had called an emergency meeting to discuss plans for her birthday party. "What are the choices again?" Robin said.

"Bowling in town and Dairy Queen," said Kim.

"Town" was what everyone called One Hundred Mile House, which was just under an hour's drive from Bridge Lake. For big things, Robin's family went to Kamloops, but for groceries and the occasional meal at a restaurant, they went to One Hundred Mile House.

"We went bowling at Jenna's party," said Bryn. "How about the Canada Games pool in Kamloops?"

"Too far," said Kayla. "Unless we can stay overnight in a hotel?" she added hopefully.

Kim sighed. "Not a chance."

"How many games would we get to play if we went bowling?" said Bryn.

"Don't know," said Kim.

The girls fell silent. Robin stood up. What were Mom and April *doing*? She'd gone to the office and phoned home at recess and at the beginning of lunch hour. No answer. "I'll be right back," she said.

The answering machine wasn't working, and Robin let the phone ring thirty-four times. Then she gave up.

The bell rang just as she got back to the classroom. She slid into her desk.

Kim turned around. "We decided on a sleepover," she said.

Surprise, surprise.

Robin grinned. "Good."

"I always have a sleepover," sighed Kim.

"I know," said Robin. "That's what's so good about it. Movies?"

"I think I can talk them into three. Two for night and one for morning."

"Perfect."

✳

Mom was in a good mood. She was humming as Robin and Molly clambered over grocery bags into the backseat of the station wagon. The worry line between her eyebrows had disappeared. And she didn't erupt when Molly peered hopefully into one of the bags and said, "Did you get me anything?"

"There just might be a Kinder Surprise in one of those bags," said Mom.

"I didn't know you were going to town," Robin blurted out.

"We didn't know either," said Mom lightly. "It was spur of the moment. Based on the sad contents of the fridge and cupboards."

Mom was exaggerating. Things weren't that bad at home. Usually everyone had lots of notice before a trip to One Hundred Mile House so they could add things to the list that lived on the fridge.

April spoke for the first time. "Are we going to tell them what happened at lunch?"

Mom's mouth twitched. "I thought we were going to keep that a secret."

Molly leaned forward like Jellybean smelling a mouse. "What happened?"

"Well…it was kind of embarrassing." Mom was grinning widely now.

"You have to tell!" yelled Molly. "That's the rule when you start something."

Robin scowled. Of course Mom was going to tell. If Molly wasn't so dumb, she'd know that. The car felt crowded with grocery bags and little sisters.

"Okay," said Mom. "April and I went to Luigi's for lunch."

Luigi's was a new restaurant in One Hundred Mile House. Robin had only got as far as peering through the window at the tables with fancy red tablecloths and candles in bottles. Mom had promised to take Robin with her the first time she tried it out.

"We'd finished eating and Aunty Jen was reading a newspaper," said April.

"I was checking ads for tractor parts for your Dad and—"

"It caught on fire!"

"I dipped it too close to the candle." Mom started to laugh.

Molly's eyes were as round as marbles. "Did you stop, drop and roll?" she asked. "That's what we learned at school."

"The paper was on fire, not us. The waiter grabbed it and ran out of the restaurant, holding it. I think he panicked." Mom was laughing too hard to finish. "You tell the rest, April."

April turned around and grinned at Robin and Molly. "Aunty Jen said, 'But I haven't finished reading it yet!'"

That was it? Mom was killing herself laughing because she'd almost set a restaurant on fire? Robin's face felt cold.

Molly slumped back against the seat. "Can I take April for my show-and-tell?"

Robin stared at her. "What's that got to do with the fire?"

"Nothing," said Molly. "I just need a better show-and-tell than Sally Penner. She brought her brother's lizard."

Robin snorted.

Mom said, "Oh, Molly girl, I missed you."

Mom and April burst out laughing again. Robin frowned, shifting her thoughts away, and concentrated instead on her plans for training Kedar.

Chapter Five

Robin had to wait all weekend to have April to herself. While more snow fell outside, Friday night and most of Saturday had been taken up by an endless family game of Monopoly. Dad had declared himself King of Boardwalk and had torn up little pieces of red napkin to make extra hotels.

There was one bad moment early Saturday morning when April discovered that their Internet connection wasn't working and probably wouldn't be fixed for a week or two.

"How am I supposed to talk to my friends?" she had wailed. It wasn't that big a deal, but April turned it into one. Robin even heard her telling Gran about it during her nightly phone call.

The news from Gran on Saturday night was about the same. Aunty Liz had stabilized, but no one quite knew what came next. Sunday morning Dad left when it was still dark to do his *rain-hail-sleet-and-snow* thing. Molly's friend's mother picked her up for a play day, and Mom retreated to her bedroom with fierce warnings that she was not to be disturbed "unless the chimney is on fire, the water pipes burst or there is a major appliance failure."

Over bowls of cereal, Robin tried to decide how to approach April with her idea. April didn't want to make plans, but this would be fun. Finally she took a big breath and burst out, "Why don't we ski to the cabin? Dad says I'm allowed, as long as I let someone know I'm going there."

April hesitated, and Robin was sure she was going to say no. Then she shrugged. "Yeah, okay, though I won't be able to ski as fast as you."

The cabin was behind the ridge on the other side of the lake. It had belonged to a trapper and had been abandoned fifty years earlier. Dad had fixed it up before Robin was born, patching holes in the roof, adding a porch and repairing the metal chimney. He had carried in supplies on horseback, and Robin's family liked to go there for picnics or to warm up on snowshoe or cross-country-ski trips.

Robin filled her fanny pack with oatmeal cookies and two Japanese oranges left over from Christmas. She scribbled a quick note for Mom.

The girls laced up their ski boots, grabbed tuques and mitts and headed outside. They stepped into their skis and slid down the slope to the lake. Robin squinted in the brightness and checked out the old ski track. All that was left in the fresh snow was a faint ridge. She set off across the bay, pushing herself hard. She sucked in gulps of cold air and let everything slide out of her mind. Sometimes breaking a new ski trail was like plowing through wet cement, but today the snow was powdery and fast.

When she reached the far shore, she waited. April looked small and far away. It was easy to imagine the house wasn't there and to pretend that they were the only travelers on a vast snowy tundra. They used to play this game all the time. Inuit hunters, struggling to reach their camp...

She decided to take a chance. "We have to keep going, Ootpik," she gasped as April caught up. "Polar bear...behind the island...no bullets left."

"Any provisions left?" puffed April, and Robin felt herself relax.

"I ate the last frozen fish, but there's always our bootlaces. We could eat those."

"Aaargh!" said April.

"We'll head for the igloo," said Robin.

The igloo was the snow-covered abandoned beaver lodge in the bay at the end of the lake. The girls took off their skis and stuck them in the snow and then climbed to the top of the mound.

"Remember sliding down this when we were little kids?" said April suddenly. "It seemed so big."

"Yeah. Even Molly's outgrown it now." Robin touched April's arm. "Look."

A moose had stepped out of a clump of willow trees. He stood very still and stared at the girls, as if trying to figure out what they were. Then he loped through the deep snow along the shoreline, his long legs reminding Robin of an ungainly giraffe. With one last look back, he scrambled up the bank and disappeared into the trees.

April shivered. "It's so lonely out here."

Robin never felt that way. She loved the lake in the winter. She searched the shoreline for the split pine tree that marked the beginning of the cabin trail. "Let's go!"

The girls put theirs skis back on and skied to the shore, and then they started to climb up a steep hillside. The snow was deeper and softer here. Robin checked for blazes on the trees to make sure they were going the right way.

At the top of the hill, she leaned on her poles, panting, and whooped, "We made it!" Below her, the trees opened into a sloping meadow. At the bottom was a long, narrow, snow-covered pond with a small cabin tucked at one end.

April shoved off with her poles and shouted, "Race you!"

It was like skiing through clouds. The powdery snow floated around Robin's knees. Her cheeks stung with the cold. Perfect!

They skied almost to the door of the cabin. They stuck their poles and skis in the snow, and Robin tugged on the door. *Oomph!* It clung stubbornly for a few seconds and then gave in with a grunt.

It seemed colder inside than outside. There was a table and two wooden chairs, an old black woodstove and wooden bunks with sleeping bags stored underneath in plastic bins. A board shelf was cluttered with dishes, a lantern, some tins of food and a smoke-blackened pot.

In the end, they decided to eat their cookies and oranges outside in the sun, stamping a flat place in the snow with their skis.

They munched in silence for a few minutes. Then Robin licked the last bit of orange juice off her fingers and gathered up the peels. April leaned back against a big spruce tree and closed her eyes.

A sudden picture of Aunty Liz hit Robin with a jolt. Last Christmas, they had all skied to the cabin. Aunty Liz had been resting against that same tree where April was now. Molly had crept up with a mitten full of snow and slid it down Aunty Liz's jacket. Robin could still hear her pretended roar of rage.

Robin shivered. Would Aunty Liz be able to ski again? Would she even be able to walk? Nervously, she sorted through the jumble of information in her head.

She didn't know much. It had been a horrible accident. People had been killed. No one had told her anything else.

Okay, be fair. She hadn't exactly demanded to know. But this was the first time she and April had been alone. Molly was a pest all day. And in the evenings, April talked to Mom. Snatches of their conversations poked at Robin like pins. Traction. Crushed pelvis. Screws. It made her stomach feel queasy.

Robin scooped up snow in her mitten and tried to put together a question. She turned words around in her head. They felt like they were stuck together like chewing gum. She couldn't just blurt out, "Will Aunty Liz be able to ski again?" April would feel horrible. And it wouldn't change anything.

It was too hard to talk about. "You know what would be fun?" she said instead. "To come up here by ourselves and stay the night."

"Would we be allowed?" said April doubtfully.

"There's a chance." Robin's mind was already formulating ideas.

The girls worked out the details as they climbed to the top of the ridge. Baked beans or soup? Hot chocolate for sure. Marshmallows. They could roast them in the woodstove. Monopoly? It was no fun with two people. Cards would be better. And definitely some books.

The ski back down the hill was fast and fun on the newly packed ski trail. As the girls headed across the lake to the house, they talked about their chances of an overnighter. Dad might go for it, but Mom was definitely a problem. They'd have to work on her.

Making plans.

Robin felt like singing at the top of her lungs. It was like old times—before April got that closed look in her eyes. Before the accident.

Chapter Six

Robin approached Mom and Dad with their idea during supper. When she ran out of arguments, she looked at April for backup, but April was playing with her salad. She looked tired.

"I don't know—," Mom began.

"You always do this!" Robin burst out.

"Do what?" said Mom.

"Get this look on your face. And then come up with a hundred things that could go wrong that never do."

Mom looked offended. "I don't think that's true."

"It is a little," said Dad, grinning. "Never mind. Every family needs one worrywart. I, for one, think it's a good idea."

Robin had been prepared for a fight. She clamped her mouth shut and held her breath. Mom frowned.

"They can take the walkie talkie with them," said Dad. He sounded enthusiastic. "They could call if they ran into trouble. I could be up there in twenty minutes on the snowmobile if they needed me."

"Which we won't," said Robin.

Mom sighed. "Do they have to do this right now, with everything that's been happening?"

"That's exactly why they should do it now," said Dad. Robin felt like leaping up and hugging him.

Molly's head had swiveled back and forth as she followed the conversation. "I'm going too," she said.

"No," said Robin. "It's just going to be me and April."

Molly's face turned bright red. "That's not fair!"

"Life isn't always fair," said Mom automatically.

"But I never get to do anything fun!"

Molly sounded like she was settling in for a long siege. Robin turned to Mom and said loudly, "Well?"

"When?" said Mom, giving in.

"Saturday," said Robin. They could come home from Kim's party right after lunch and go.

After supper, Dad offered to do the dishes. "Temporary goodwill, girls. Take advantage of it."

"Hot bubble bath for me," said Mom.

"Saxophone," said April. "I've hardly done any practicing yet."

Robin grabbed her jacket off its hook. She had to feed the horses, and then she was free. "You want to help me, Molly?"

Molly made a face. "I'm staying with April."

"If you're quiet," said April.

Robin grinned. She wrapped her scarf mummy-style around her face. Molly quiet? When polar bears could fly.

The bellow came just as Robin was about to leave. "I did not!"

Dad turned around at the sink. Molly stormed into the kitchen, her face as red as a tomato. April hung in the doorway, her eyes cold. "That's weird because I left it leaning against the computer table *in* its case and now it's on the bed *out* of its case."

Robin froze at the door. What was this all about? April looked furious.

"I didn't touch it." Molly sidled closer to Dad.

"Oh, pardon me. It must have been Jellybean. Or Hurly. I guess he decided to try my sax."

Molly started to giggle and then looked at April's face. "I didn't break it or anything," she mumbled into Dad's stomach.

Dad pushed Molly gently away. "Molly?"

"I didn't hurt it. I was just looking at it."

"That saxophone cost a lot of money," said April. "And I'd also like a bit of privacy."

"I agree," said Dad. "Molly, from now on April's room is out-of-bounds, unless you're invited. And you owe April an apology."

Molly stiffened. "I'm glad I touched it!"

"Molly."

"I said I'M GLAD I TOUCHED IT!" yelled Molly.

"Hey!" said Dad. "Off to your room, young lady!"

Molly let her breath out with a noisy explosion. She burst into loud sobs and ran out of the kitchen.

"Sorry about that, April," said Dad.

April frowned. "I just don't like people going in my room, that's all."

Robin bit her lip. She waited for Dad to say something. He was scrubbing a pan with a Brillo pad, humming through his teeth. A sure sign he was bugged. Was he mad at April or at Molly? Robin wasn't sure. She slipped outside and shut the door.

After she had put out the hay, she lingered by the corral, reluctant to go back inside. The geldings drifted like shadows between the piles of hay. Then they settled down to a smooth rhythmic chewing.

Robin tilted her face to the starry sky, searching for planets. She tried to bring back the feeling she'd had when she and April were skiing.

Talking, making plans. Like old times.

But the feeling was gone, like when Molly made a picture on her magic slate and then pulled the plastic sheet. All that was left was an empty gray hole.

On Monday morning, the school bus presented a problem. The driver, Mr. Thomas, hadn't even come to a stop, and already Robin could see Kim through the window, rearranging herself to make room. Robin and Kim *always* sat together. Robin's stomach tightened.

Then April said, "Oh yeah, I promised Molly I'd sit with her," and Robin sagged with relief. Sometimes it was handy to have a younger sister.

When they got to school, Robin took April to the office to register. Then she led her down to the grade-five classroom. She showed her the empty desk beside hers. "Kim's right behind me. You know her. And Bryn's in front of you and Sarah's behind you. You'll like them."

April didn't look like she was listening. She was digging in her backpack.

"Have you got everything you need?" said Robin.

"For the hundredth time, yes." April pulled out notebooks and a handful of loose pens.

First period was math. Mr. Nordoff passed out a worksheet on multiplying and dividing fractions. It was easy. Robin flew through the questions. She glanced sideways at April.

April was gripping her pencil, but she wasn't doing anything. Just sitting there. Worry began to gnaw at Robin's stomach.

She dropped her eraser and then leaned over to pick it up. On the way back up, she had a good look at April's paper. She had written her name and had doodled in the corner. That was it. Robin's stomach sank. April's class probably hadn't got to fractions yet. It wasn't fair to expect her to just walk in and do the work.

Robin glanced at the front of the room. Mr. Nordoff was busy marking a stack of papers. She took a big breath. She leaned over and slid her paper onto April's desk.

April froze for a second. Then she started to copy the answers, with a tiny frown on her face.

It was very quiet in the room, just the rustling of Mr. Nordoff's papers and a few scattered sighs and shifting chairs. Mr. Nordoff put down his marking pen and glanced up. Robin's heart gave a jump. She leaned over and shielded her desk with her arms. She held her breath.

For one hopeful second, she thought that Mr. Nordoff had gone back to his marking. Then she heard the scrape of his chair and his footsteps as he walked down the aisle.

April stopped writing and sat very still. Mr. Nordoff stopped beside her desk. He picked up both papers and said in a quiet voice, "If you need help, next time ask."

April's face turned scarlet. Lots of the kids turned around and stared. Robin kept her eyes on the top of her desk. Misery welled inside her.

Mr. Nordoff went back to the front of the room. He dropped the two worksheets on his desk. "Ten more minutes," he said.

The minutes crept by. It was mortifying sitting there with nothing to do. Robin slid her ruler out of her desk and studied the numbers. She peeked sideways at April. Her face was burning, and she was looking at her hands.

When the class monitors collected the papers, Robin pretended not to care that she didn't have one. She made herself busy, scooping up loose pencil shavings from the front of her desk and putting them in her pencil box.

When the lunch bell rang, April muttered, "I'm going to the washroom."

"I—," began Robin.

"I *know* the way," said April.

Robin made her lunch last as long as possible. She kept one eye on the door. Soon everyone else had headed outside or to the computer lab, except for Kim, who pulled her chair up beside Robin's and unwrapped a package of cheese and crackers. She settled comfortably into her favorite topic, her birthday party. "So, what do you want? Hawaiian or pepperoni?"

"What?"

"The pizza. For...the...party." Kim spoke in an exaggerated slow voice.

"I don't care."

Where had April gone? No one could take that long in the washroom. And she would be starving by now, because she had refused to eat anything for breakfast.

"I guess I'll ask for both kinds," sighed Kim. "And Bryn's bringing CDs. She's got the most."

"April has lots of CDs," said Robin.

An odd look flickered across Kim's face. Suddenly she seemed to be concentrating very hard on folding her waxed paper.

"I'll ask her to bring them," Robin said.

"She's not invited," said Kim in a low voice.

Robin felt like she'd been kicked. "What?"

Kim glanced at the door. "I can only have five people."

"You never said that before."

"It's Mom's new rule. And she means it. And anyway, I never said that April was invited. You just assumed…" Kim's voice trailed away.

"Of course I *assumed*. April is my cousin and she's living with me."

"Really. I hadn't heard." Kim's face was white.

Robin felt rigid with anger. "I don't believe this. You know what the problem is? You don't like April. You never have."

"April's okay," said Kim slowly. "Though you can't exactly call her friendly. But I just want kids that I know really well at my party."

Robin's heart started to pound. "That's mean."

"Then I'm mean," said Kim. "I'm going outside."

She made a lot of noise packing up her lunch stuff, and then she was gone.

Robin swallowed. She couldn't believe what had just happened.

Fine. If April wasn't going to the party, she wasn't going either. It was that simple.

Robin tested the idea in her head. She felt sick. She stuffed the rest of her lunch back in her bag and went in search of her cousin.

＊

In last period, Mr. Nordoff announced a special project.

"It's called imagery. Words that mean something different than they say. We use imagery all the time without even thinking about it. When we say things like, *The cat's got your tongue. You drive me up the wall. I caught your eye.*"

Robin had a sinking feeling that this was not going to be an ordinary project. Mr. Nordoff produced an ice-cream pail full of strips of paper. "I've written an image on each piece of paper. You may work alone or with a partner. I want you to represent your image any way you can. A poster. A model. Be creative. You have one week."

Kim seemed to have forgotten she was mad. She poked Robin's back. Robin's stomach tightened. The poke meant *Don't forget we're partners.* Kim plunged into projects with an enthusiasm that usually ended up being a lot of work, but Robin couldn't imagine working with anyone else. But what about April?

There were a lot of groans as kids took turns pulling out the strips of paper.

"Don't tell!" said Mr. Nordoff, bouncing around like a kid at a birthday party. "We'll all try to guess the images when the projects are finished."

Robin felt Kim's eyes burning into her back. Beside her, April was digging holes in her eraser with her pencil. She looked bored.

Robin put her hand up. "Is it okay if we work in groups of three?"

Mr. Nordoff frowned. "That never works. One person ends up doing nothing."

"But—"

Robin sank back in her chair. Sweat prickled her back. The ice-cream pail went up and down the aisles. There was a lot of chatter mixed with groans. Then the pail stopped in front of April. She swept the bits of eraser into a pile and glanced at Robin. "If you don't mind, I'll work by myself."

Relief flooded Robin. But she had to make sure. "I could ask again—"

"I like working by myself," said April. She pulled out a piece of paper, read it with an expressionless face and said nothing.

Kim chose for her and Robin. *Castles in the air,* said the slip of paper. Robin frowned. What was that supposed to mean?

The bell rang and Kim said happily, "We can brainstorm ideas on the bus."

"Sure," said Robin.

She slid another glance at April. Her cousin had said she liked working by herself. She didn't look upset. So why was Robin so sure that she was lying?

Chapter Seven

The next morning on the bus, Kim announced, "I looked up *castles in the air* on the Internet."

"What?" said Robin.

"Castles in the air. Our project that we have one week to do. In case you've forgotten."

"I haven't forgotten." Robin's eyes felt like they were stuck together. She had been awake most of the night, tossing and turning, worrying about Kim's stupid birthday party. How was she ever going to get the nerve to tell Kim she wasn't going?

"It's an expression," said Kim. "Mom's heard of it."

Robin looked at her blankly.

"Castles in the air. Oh, forget it." Kim slumped back in her seat.

"Sorry." Robin pulled her mind away from the party to easier ground. Kim always got in a flap about projects, and they always came up with something good at the end. "I'm listening now. Honestly."

Kim dug a piece of paper out of her pocket. "I wrote it down because I wasn't really sure if I got it." She frowned. "It means something that's not realistic."

"*What*?" said Robin.

"Mom said it's like when you have dreams, but they don't have a chance of working out because they're not realistic. That's called building castles in the air."

Both girls were silent. Robin made an effort to focus. "Poster or papier-mâché?" she said finally.

"Everyone does that. I want to do something different," said Kim.

"Remember the last time we tried to do something different?" said Robin darkly. "Aardvark. Exactly six lines in the encyclopedia. We could have picked chimpanzee or leopard."

"I bet it's worth a lot of marks," moaned Kim.

"We'll go to the library at lunchtime," said Robin. "Don't worry. We'll come up with something."

✳

"I give up," said Kim. "We need to change topics."

"Bryn and Kayla already tried that, but Mr. Nordoff said no," said Robin. "He said to think of it as a challenge."

The girls sat at one of the library tables, surrounded by a mountain of books about castles and the Middle Ages. Kim had rejected Robin's last idea of building a castle out of cardboard and sticking it on a cloud made of cotton balls.

"What's wrong with it?" Robin had demanded.

"I don't know. I just don't want to do that."

For a fleeting moment, Robin wondered what April's slip of paper had said. Did she really not care that she didn't have a partner? Most of the fun of doing projects was working with someone. Robin had invited her to come to the library with them at lunch hour, but April had muttered something about talking to the art teacher and then disappeared.

"And when are we going to get together to work on this thing anyway? We can't do it Friday because of my party." Kim was sliding into a full-scale panic. "Maybe you can stay at my house Saturday night too?"

An icicle slid down Robin's back. Saturday night was the overnight at the cabin. And Robin wasn't going to be at Kim's party on Friday anyway. Do it now, a voice whispered in her ear. Just tell her. *I'm not going to your party.*

"Do you think you could stay two nights?" Kim looked at her hopefully.

Robin swallowed. "Maybe," she said.

That night Dad barbecued. Robin stood beside him on the porch in her down parka, her hands buried in warm oven mitts. "Why are we doing this?"

"Why not?" Dad poured a stream of red barbecue sauce across the steaks.

"It's winter." Robin stamped her boots to keep warm.

"Hey! You're jiggling everything!" Dad stabbed one of the steaks with the end of a knife. "I think we'll go for well-done tonight."

Molly stuck her head out the kitchen door. "Mom wants to know how much longer."

"Five minutes."

"April says steak is gross," Molly announced. "She says that cows have a right to live, just like us."

"Scat, rat, you're letting all the cold air in the house."

April must have come out of her room at last, thought Robin. Her cousin had brought home a plastic bag of old magazines that the art teacher had given her and had shut herself up in the computer room as soon as they got home.

"Done," said Dad, poking another steak. Hurly circled his feet, and he pushed him away with his boot. "I'd like to know who's been teaching this dog to beg."

"Dad?"

"Yup."

"Did these steaks come from one of Kim's family's cows?"

"Yes. What's the matter? You're not going over to the other side too, are you?"

"No," said Robin firmly.

At the dinner table, Molly turned down steak and munched her way through a baked potato and carrot sticks. Robin took a bite of meat and tried to decide if she felt guilty. Chew chew. Nope. Nothing.

Partway through the meal, the phone rang.

"I'll get it!" Molly dived for the phone. "It's Gran," she reported. "Guess what, Gran? My tooth is coming out...a loonie, I hope...Here's Mom."

Robin swirled her milk in the bottom of her glass. This was an odd time for Gran to phone. She usually called around eight, when she got back from the hospital. She glanced at April. April had stopped eating and was staring at the phone.

"I see." Mom's voice was smooth. "I think I'll take this in the other room. It's a little noisy in here."

It wasn't noisy at all, thought Robin, unless you counted the clink of knives and forks. Even that had stopped for a few seconds, and then Dad started in on a story about a fox he'd seen while he was plowing.

Mom was gone a long time. Robin was scraping plates into the garbage, and Dad was dishing up tapioca pudding when she came back. She slipped into her chair and stared at her half-eaten dinner.

"Everything okay?" said Dad.

"Ye-es. There's been a bit of a complication." Mom looked directly at April. "It's nothing to worry about. The doctors want to do a little more surgery on your mother."

"What do you mean?" said April. Her face went pale.

"They need to put in another pin."

"Doesn't sound too serious," said Dad.

"No, it's not. It's just slowing things down a little. Frankly, I'm worried about Gran. She's exhausted. It's two bus transfers every time she goes to the hospital. I don't mean that she doesn't want to go," she added quickly. "It's just that she sounds so tired."

Dad slid Mom's plate away and set down a bowl of tapioca. "Why don't you fly down for the weekend?"

Mom made a little humming noise. Robin could tell she was digging in her mind for complications.

Dad steamed ahead. "I'm off tomorrow morning. I could take you to the airport in Kamloops first thing, and you could fly back on Monday."

"That might work," said Mom.

"Otherwise you'll just sit here and worry."

"Can I go with you?" said April. "Please."

"You can't!" said Robin instantly. "We're staying overnight at the cabin on Saturday!"

As soon as she said it, she realized how horrible it sounded. Like she didn't care about Aunty Liz at all. And she did. "I mean—"

April gave her a frozen look. Then she turned back to Mom. "Please, Aunty Jen. She's *my* mother."

Mom glanced at Dad. He shook his head slightly. Mom said slowly, "Not this time, honey."

"*Please!*"

"You just got here," said Dad. "You're just getting settled in at school."

"I'd only miss a few days. I could make it up."

"It's not a good idea this time," said Mom softly. She reached out for April's hand. April pushed herself away from the table. With a small cry, she stood up and ran out of the room. A few seconds later, the computer-room door slammed.

Mom gave Dad a drowning look. "*Are* we being unfair?"

"If April goes with you now, she won't want to come back," said Dad. "And that's going to create a whole new set of problems."

Robin felt something cold and hard in her stomach.

Molly's eyes widened. "Why won't she—?"

"Shut up, Molly!" said Robin.

"Hey!" said Dad. "Enough of that kind of talk, Robin!"

"About this overnight at the cabin," said Mom. "I'd feel better about it if I were here. I think the girls can wait until next week."

"*What?*" said Robin.

"Agreed," said Dad.

The notes of April's saxophone drifted through the house. Robin pushed back angry tears and stirred her tapioca slowly. She took a big, steadying breath.

"It looks like fish eggs," she said in a loud voice. "Now that's gross."

Chapter Eight

Robin dug out some of her Christmas bubble bath and retreated to the tub with a book. Three pages into her chapter, she could sense Molly hovering outside the bathroom door.

"Molly, scram."

"You promised you'd play Madeline tonight. Nobody ever plays Madeline—"

"Ask April."

"She's in her room, and she locked the door."

Robin squeezed a handful of bubbles and watched them seep between her fingers.

"Pleeeeeease."

Robin made a huffing sound. "I want to read one whole chapter without being bugged."

"I'll wait."

"Not there. I can hear you breathing."

"I'll be in my room. But don't forget."

Robin slid into *Hatchet*. It was great, about a boy who crashed an airplane in the wilderness. All he had was a hatchet his mom had given him, and he had to learn how to survive. Food, shelter, fire—easy problems. Robin sighed. She wouldn't mind trading places with him right now.

When the water was lukewarm and Robin's fingers had wrinkled up like soft raisins, she remembered Molly. Guiltily she pulled the plug and got into her dressing gown.

Molly's bedroom door was three-quarters shut. "I'm here," said Robin. "Sorry, Mol."

"Shh," said Molly in a cross voice. She was bent over her blue dolls' bed. "Visiting hours in the hospital are over. You'll wake Aunty Liz."

Robin stared at the plastic doll tucked under a baby blanket. One eye was missing its eyelashes, the yellow hair was sparse in patches and the pink plastic face was crisscrossed with Pocahontas Band-Aids.

"I picked my most wrecked doll," said Molly. "Do you think a real hospital would have Pocahontas Band-Aids?"

Robin swallowed her shock. "Um...why not?"

"Do you think that's too many Band-Aids? April says that Aunty Liz has a lot of Band-Aids."

Bandages, Robin mentally corrected. She bit her lip. Band-Aids were for small unimportant things—scraped knees and slivers. "I think you've got just the right amount."

Molly gently pulled the blanket back. Pieces of white felt from her craft bin were taped around the doll's legs. "These are the casts," she explained. "Two of them, right up to her hip. And this is her...pelvic bone." Molly stumbled over the unfamiliar word. "It's broken in three places. That's where the pins are. And the something bone is crushed. We're also worried about her kidneys."

Robin stared at Molly. "How do you know all that?"

"April told me." Molly frowned. "I don't know how to pretend the traction. That's kind of like...pulleys. I need some string or something. Do you think traction hurts a lot?"

Suddenly tears slid down Molly's flushed cheeks. Robin pulled her little sister toward her and wrapped her arms around her. "I don't think it hurts too much," she whispered.

Molly was shivering hard. "Will Aunty Liz get better?"

"Yes."

"Why is April mad at everybody?"

Robin closed her eyes, trying to shut out the pounding in her head. "April's not really mad. She misses Aunty Liz, that's all. Like we miss Mom when she goes away."

Molly said, "Dad says if April went away, she wouldn't come back. Did he mean forever?"

"Not forever." Robin squeezed Molly's thin shoulders. "And besides, Dad's wrong."

"I'm not coming to your party."

Robin had given Kim three whole days to change her mind and invite April. It hadn't happened. And now, on the bus on the way to school, Robin told her.

"Pardon me?" said Kim coldly.

"I'm...not...coming. I can't. Not if you're not inviting April."

There. Even Kim should get that.

She did. She stared at Robin in disbelief. Then she said, "Fine!" and turned her shoulder to the window. They rode the rest of the way to school in a silence as cold as icicles.

✳

Robin thought the day would never end. It was well below zero outside, and Mr. Nordoff let everyone stay inside at lunch hour.

Lots of the kids worked on their projects. The room quickly became a sea of colored paper. Everyone seemed to have a partner except April who was working quietly at her desk, cutting pictures out of a magazine.

How could you work on a project with someone who wasn't talking to you? Robin buried herself in a book, ignoring Kim and Bryn and Kayla, who were huddled in a corner of the room, giggling.

The hollow feeling in her stomach deepened when she got home. Mom had gone to Vancouver in the morning, leaving behind a big hole in the house. Molly flopped in front of the TV, and April retreated to the computer room with her magazines, a shoe box that Dad had given her and some poster paint. Robin headed out to the horse corrals to visit Kedar.

✳

After supper, while she and April loaded the dishwasher, Robin said, "I could help you with your project. I won't tell anyone what it is."

She pretended she didn't care what April's answer was. She poured the dishwasher soap into its cup, her heart pounding.

April shrugged. "Sure. Mr. Nordoff said it's supposed to be a secret, but it's not a big deal."

"We got *castles in the air*," said Robin, relieved. "Kim says it kind of means things that aren't realistic."

"That one's hard." April sounded sympathetic, and Robin felt the tight knot in her shoulders relax. "Mine's easier. *Down in the dumps.* How are you and Kim doing?"

Robin considered telling her that they weren't doing well at all; in fact, they weren't doing anything. "We're still trying to decide what to make," she said.

Robin followed April to the computer room and glanced around curiously. She hadn't been in here once since her cousin had moved in. If you could call it moving in. April had hardly made a mark on the room. There were a few clothes laid neatly across a chair, her saxophone sat in front of the hide-a-bed and her duffel bag lay in a corner of the room, unzipped and still full of clothes. Robin was pretty sure the dresser drawers were empty.

The *Welcome April* poster looked dumb now. Embarrassed, Robin examined the shoe box which sat on the desk. April had divided the inside into halves and painted one half blue and one half black. "So what exactly are you doing?" Robin said.

She listened, impressed, while April explained her idea. In the black side of the box, she was constructing a miniature garbage dump. She had cut out tiny pictures of clothes, a refrigerator, a TV, cereal boxes and toys and had glued them onto a sheet of poster board. Then she had cut them out again carefully. "I'm going to stick them all together so they look like a pile of garbage," she finished.

"Neat," said Robin. She thought of the local dump where Dad took their garbage every two weeks. There was always lots of old stuff piled up. "Maybe you could find a picture of a couch," she suggested.

"I saw a couch that looked practically brand new at the dump once."

"That's a good idea," said April. She tossed a pile of magazines on the bed. "You can look through these for sad faces. That's what I'm putting on the blue side. Get it? That's what *down in the dumps* means. Feeling sad."

Robin wondered if this was the best thing for April to be doing. Wouldn't a bunch of sad faces make her feel even worse? But April was humming as she worked on her pile of garbage. Robin stretched out on the bed and thumbed through the pages.

There were a lot more happy faces than sad faces in a magazine, she quickly discovered. But it was fun looking. Every time she found a sad face, she shouted, "Got one!" and cut it out.

After a while, she stood up and peered over April's shoulder. The miniature garbage dump looked perfect. She wondered glumly if there was any chance Mr. Nordoff would let her switch partners.

April leaned back and stretched. "I'm going to the bathroom. I'll be back in a minute."

Robin had used up her pile of magazines. She started rummaging through the stack on the edge of the desk, looking for one that looked like it had lots of people in it. A piece of paper stuck between two magazines slid onto the floor.

She picked it up and examined it. Her heart gave a funny little jump. It was a letter to Stephanie.

Robin glanced at the door and then turned back to the paper. She scanned it quickly, her heart racing.

Dear Stephanie,

I have to write to you because there's no Internet here. It sucks. Everything about this place sucks. The school is tiny and boring. There's nothing to do. No after-school clubs or anything because everyone goes home on the bus. Robin is acting weird. I MISS YOU. All I want to do is come home. Did you ever get a chance to ask your parents if I could stay with you while Mom's in the hospital? PLEASE PLEASE PLEASE beg them—

"I promised Molly we'd both play Madeline and—what are you doing?"

Robin dropped the letter on the desk and spun around. She felt like she had been kicked hard in the stomach.

April stared at the piece of paper. Recognition flashed through her eyes and the color drained from her face.

"How dare you—" Robin swallowed. The words threatened to choke her. "How *dare* you say those things!"

For a second, April hesitated. Then she blazed, "How dare you read my letter! It's none of your business!"

"You practically left it in plain sight." Robin's hands started to shake. "I can't believe you would say all that."

"That's because you don't believe anything you don't want to!"

"What's that supposed to mean?"

"This. Everything. You act like this is supposed to be some big holiday. Like nothing has changed."

Robin's legs felt like jelly. "That's not fair! I don't think that!"

April's eyes narrowed. "Maybe everything I said in the letter isn't true, but most of it is! I hate being here. Do you get that? I *hate* being here. I want to be in Vancouver with my mother!"

Robin felt like she couldn't breathe.

"And you can stop pretending that I don't know about Kim's stupid party tomorrow night. Don't stay home for my sake!"

Fighting with April was way worse than fighting with Kim. Kim would go all silent and cold, but she never said cruel things. Robin drew herself up. "Don't worry," she said icily. "I have no intention of missing it!"

She stormed out of the room and slammed the door behind her.

Chapter Nine

The next morning, Robin lugged a garbage bag containing a sleeping bag, a pillow and pajamas onto the school bus. For one breathless moment, Kim's face registered complete shock, and then she grinned and said, "Mom rented four movies yesterday!"

Robin sank gratefully into her seat. That was another reason it was easier to fight with Kim. She forgave quickly. April was still furious. She had ignored Robin all morning and had been coldly polite to Dad. She was sitting in an empty seat at the back of the bus now, reading a book.

"Did you ask if you could stay two nights?" said Kim.

"I'm not allowed. Mom's gone back to Vancouver, and Dad said it would look like I'm ignoring April." The misery that had been sitting in Robin's stomach all morning welled up. "Not that it makes any difference if I'm there or not."

"What do you mean?" Kim looked eager for information.

"She just stays in her room anyway, working on her stupid project or playing her saxophone."

There was an uncomfortable silence. Robin wished she could take back what she had just said. It made her feel disloyal. For a moment, she thought about the old plan to spend Saturday night at the cabin. She was surprised to realize that she didn't even feel mad at Mom anymore for wrecking things. Besides, it would never have worked anyway. Dad had pointed out this morning that there was supposed to be frigid Arctic air and a blizzard coming in on Saturday afternoon.

Robin tried to put together a new plan. "You could come over to my place on Sunday, and we could work on our project then."

"Will April be there?"

"Of course." Robin could hear the stiffness in her own voice.

"I guess so."

Robin took a big breath and said, "So, tell me what movies you got."

✳

As far as parties went, Kim's birthday was a success. It revolved around junk food, talking and movies, which is exactly how parties should be, Robin thought. The problem was her. She just wasn't in the mood.

She drifted through the evening, laughing when the others laughed, pretending to be interested when Jenna described the new boy who had joined her Highland dancing class, and even stuffing down a slice of pizza and half a Coke, though she wasn't one bit hungry.

When they had enough energy left for only one more movie, Robin slid gratefully into her sleeping bag. It was easier to be quiet, not to have to pretend, to lie there and let the movie float over her.

"Great," she agreed with the others when it was finally over and everyone was sleepy-eyed and fighting yawns. "Excellent." Though she couldn't remember a single thing that had happened.

She slipped upstairs to ask Kim's mother, Audrey, for a Tylenol. "It's just a little headache," she explained. "It's really not that bad, I just thought…"

She heard April's name as she stumbled back down the stairs, and then Kim's loud voice trying to cover up, "I get first dibs on the bathroom!"

Robin's headache was raging now, and she crawled back into her sleeping bag. It was almost three o'clock in the morning. Everyone at home would have gone to bed a long time ago. Tears burned behind her eyes, and she had a sudden longing to be curled up in her own bed with Jellybean purring at her feet.

Jellybean sleeps with April now, she reminded herself.

For the first time that night, she let thoughts of her cousin come in without pushing them away.

I hate being here! Do you get that? I hate being here. I want to be in Vancouver with my mother!

Robin felt sick. And then the other words that she had shoved to the back of her mind slammed into her.

You have to come, Aunty Liz. Please, please, please. I'll never ever forgive you.

Shuddering, Robin pushed her face into her pillow. A sudden, deep exhaustion washed over her like a wave, and she fell asleep in the middle of one of Bryn's long involved jokes.

When she woke up, the taste of old chips was in her mouth. Her headache was still there, though the pounding was gone. She slid out of her sleeping bag and stepped across sleeping girls to the window. The sky looked heavy and gray. Kim's father was in the driveway, bent over his truck, the hood up.

Robin glanced at her watch. It was almost noon. She stared at the girls for a moment. They were half-buried in their bags and under pillows. Without a sound, Robin pulled on her jeans and sweater. She rolled up her sleeping bag and stuffed everything in her garbage bag. Then she tiptoed upstairs.

Kim's mom was settled in front of the TV in the living room with a cup of coffee. Robin stood in the doorway for a moment. Her legs felt wobbly and her head fuzzy. "Audrey…?"

Audrey set down her cup. "Oh hi, honey. You startled me. Is everyone else up?"

"No, just me."

"I'm going to make waffles with strawberries—"

"I want to go home." Robin's voice sounded like it was coming from far away. She swallowed hard.

Audrey looked at her sharply. Then she stood up. "You don't look at all well. I'll tell Kim's dad to run you home right now if you like."

"Thank you." Robin felt dizzy with relief.

"You do your coat up. It's freezing out there today. It's dropped ten degrees in the last hour to minus fifteen. There's going to be a blizzard this afternoon."

Robin nodded. "I will. And do you think you could tell Kim I'm sorry for leaving?"

Hurly jumped all over Robin when he saw her. She put her garbage bag down on the kitchen floor and hugged him. Then she noticed the big puddle in front of the fridge. "What's going on? How come no one let you outside?"

April appeared in the doorway, her hair mussed and her face flushed. "You're back pretty early," she said, yawning.

"Hurly peed on the floor," said Robin. "And where's Dad and Molly?"

"Your dad got called to work, and I think Molly's watching TV. I went back to bed." April looked at the clock on the wall above the sink. "Wow, I've been asleep for hours! I told Molly to wake me if she needed anything."

"And she let you sleep?" Robin's chest tightened. Something was wrong. Molly never gave you a second's rest when you were babysitting her. "Molly!" she shouted.

There was no answer.

Robin stuck her head into the living room. "I thought you said she was watching TV. She's not here."

"She *was* watching TV," said April behind her.

"Like when, three hours ago? Molly! Where are you? If you're hiding, this isn't funny!"

A quick search of the house threw Robin into a complete panic. "She must be outside somewhere," she muttered. "But I don't know why she wouldn't take Hurly with her."

"You're probably getting upset over nothing," said April, but she sounded unsure. "I bet she's visiting the horses or something."

But she wasn't. While April checked the horse corrals and the barn, Robin ran through the snow to the hayshed. An icy wind had started to blow, and small hard snowflakes stung her cheeks. They met back on the porch. April was shivering, and she looked frightened. "Has she ever done this before? Just disappeared?"

"Never." And then Robin remembered. "Well, once. She was mad at everybody and said she was going to go and live in the woods. Hurly found her. She was just over where Dad was cutting firewood. But that was in the fall. She wouldn't just walk through the snow. It's too deep. And it's freezing out here."

"Would she go skiing by herself?"

"She doesn't like being cold, and besides, she's not allowed—"

"She was really upset," confessed April, her voice shaking. "She kept going on and on about why couldn't she come to the cabin with us. She said it wasn't fair."

"She never thinks anything's fair," said Robin automatically. But she felt something cold and hard in the pit of her stomach. She turned and stared at the rack of cross-country skis at the end of the porch.

Molly's skis were missing.

Chapter Ten

"It's all my fault," whispered April.

"Please stop saying that," snapped Robin. "It doesn't help." She stared out the kitchen window. It was snowing much harder now, and the branches on the trees were whipping back and forth. She peered at the thermometer through the glass. It had dipped to minus twenty.

Molly was out there somewhere. Robin's heart hammered against her ribs. "I'm going to go and look for her," she said.

"Shouldn't we try to get your dad?" said April. "He said to phone the Highways department if there was an emergency."

Robin hesitated. Dad could be miles away on his snowplow. By the time he got the message and got home, anything could have happened to Molly. "I'll phone," she said, "but I'm not going to wait until he gets here. I can't."

"I'm going with you," said April instantly.

Robin stiffened. "You don't have to."

"Yes, I do." April's voice wavered. "Molly's a good skier. She made it all the way to the cabin last year. She's probably there right now."

"She'll be freezing. And terrified." Robin found it hard to think. She gazed around wildly. What did you need to do when you went out in a blizzard?

"We'll leave a note for your dad," said April. "In case he doesn't get the message. And we should take some food. And the walkie-talkie."

Making plans. Robin felt suddenly grateful that April was here. She got the telephone number for the Highways department off the fridge and asked the man who answered to contact Dad and tell him that Molly was missing. Then she scribbled a note on a piece of paper, hesitating over the words before deciding to write: *We've gone to the cabin to get Molly. It's 1:30. We've got the radio. DON'T WORRY.*

Of course, he would worry. He'd be frantic. She stuck the note in the middle of the table. April had rummaged in the snack drawer and come up with three power bars and a bag of trail mix. Robin found the radio and slipped it in her fanny pack with the food.

Mitts. Scarves. Tuques. In a few minutes they were bundled up and ready to go.

The snowflakes were small and hard like sharp pebbles, sweeping sideways across the frozen lake. The cold bit through Robin's jacket and snow pants and stung her cheeks. She ducked her chin into her scarf and hunched her shoulders.

The ski track was still faintly visible, and the girls set out across the bay. How long until the track was buried in the new snow? Robin pushed back a wave of panic and concentrated on each stride.

Hurry!

It was impossible to know how much of a head start Molly had. Robin could hear April panting behind her, trying to keep up. Every few minutes her eyes swept the lake for a flash of purple jacket, in case Molly had turned around. Would she even see her? The island was a blurry smudge, and she couldn't see the trees on the opposite shore. It was like being inside Molly's Christmas globe.

Suddenly a gray shadow appeared beside the girls. It stood frozen for a second in the driving snow, staring at them. A coyote. It was beautiful, with thick ruffled fur and yellow eyes. Then it turned and ran, melting into the snow. It's going home to its den, thought Robin. It knows better than to stay out in this.

Doggedly she pushed on, ignoring the warnings screaming in her head. Minus twenty, the thermometer had said, but with the windchill factor it must be almost minus thirty. The ski track was completely drifted over now, and she searched desperately for landmarks. The beaver lodge…the split pine tree.

Gasping, the girls climbed up the small bank at the edge of the lake. It was darker in the forest. The wind howled high above their heads, and the tall, thin, black tree trunks swayed back and forth. Robin pulled her fingers into the palms of her hands to warm them. She clumsily tightened her grip on her poles. Her face felt like it was made out of Plasticine. Her toes were numb.

"We should have worn face masks," mumbled April. Her voice sounded stiff and different.

There were a lot of things they should have done, Robin realized, as the cold formed an icy ball inside her chest. The emergency survival pack—why had she forgotten to grab that? She thought miserably of all the things inside it—matches, a space blanket, a tiny stove…

This was stupid. They should go back. People died of hypothermia in this kind of weather.

"Keep going," said April.

She was shouting, but Robin could barely hear her above the screaming wind. She took a big breath and started to climb. Dad had marked blazes on the trees and Robin searched frantically for each one. She had skied this trail hundreds of times, but everything looked so different in the blinding snow. What time was it now? The light was flat and gray, but she had a horrible feeling it was already getting dark.

Keep going. One step at a time…Robin knew she was at the top of the ridge because suddenly the ground stopped going up. She leaned on her poles and sucked in a gulp of air. It was so cold it made her chest hurt and the inside of her nose freeze.

"We should stay together going down," said April. Her breath had formed a rime of ice around the edge of the scarf she had pulled up over her mouth. Only her eyes, wide with fear, were visible.

Robin grunted. She held out her pole. "Hang on to the end. We'll go down side by side. It's going to be slow anyway."

Robin pushed off with her other pole. It was like skiing in slow motion, plowing down the hillside through the deep snow that had drifted, in places, over their knees. Robin squeezed her eyes to slits to keep out the stinging flakes.

Cold. It was so cold.

She tried to shut out the fear growing inside her. Molly had to be at the cabin. She *had* to.

They slid to a stop on the frozen pond at the bottom of the hill. Robin had lost all sense of direction. "Go right," she said blindly.

Push, push, push, through the thick snow. April skied beside her, grunting with each stride.

A tiny break in the driving snow.

A black shape.

The cabin.

A hard gust of wind turned everything white again. And then the tip of Robin's ski hit the cabin porch with a thud.

Chapter Eleven

Molly was curled up on the bottom bunk, sobbing quietly. Her boots, tuque and purple snowsuit were caked with snow, and a trail of snow led from the door to the bunk.

Relief mingled with anger slammed into Robin. "Molly, this is the dumbest thing you've ever done!"

Molly sat up. Her sobs turned into howls.

Robin's legs felt as weak as water. She sat on the bunk beside Molly and brushed the snow from the little girl's arms and legs.

Molly gulped in air. "I'm freezing," she whimpered.

"Matches," said April. She was standing, frozen, by the door. "Where can I find matches?"

"Hang on a sec," said Robin. "We need to turn on the radio."

Robin put the radio in the middle of the table and turned the switch. "Dad, can you hear me? Dad? Dad?"

No reply. Did the radio even work in a blizzard like this? Robin had no idea. She turned and swept her eyes along the shelf. A fishing reel, a glass bottle, a box of nails, a stick curved like a snake.

Matches. In the tin can. A whole box of them.

"We're going to light the stove, Molly," said Robin. Her breath made a white cloud. "It'll warm up in here fast." She squeezed Molly's shoulders and then stumbled to her feet.

Newspaper, split logs and a few pieces of kindling were stacked beside the woodstove. The girls tugged off their mitts and with stiff fingers tore paper into strips. Robin opened the stove door, and April piled the paper in the bottom.

Robin laid all of the kindling on top of the newspaper. Her hands fumbled as she struck a match. Nothing happened. Had the matches somehow got damp? She tried again, biting down on her lip. The end of the match burst into flame, and Robin held it against the edge of the paper. The paper flared up with a reassuring *whoosh*, and then a wave of smoke swept into the cabin. Robin couldn't see the sticks or the paper anymore, just thick choking smoke.

"What happened?" coughed April.

"The damper! I forgot to open the damper," Robin grunted.

Stupid. How could she be so stupid?

Robin yanked the wire handle on the side of the black stovepipe, trying not to breathe in the smoke. The handle wouldn't budge at first but finally it turned, and the smoke cleared. She peered hopefully into the stove. The paper had turned to ashes and the sticks of kindling were charred.

"That's all the kindling we've got," said Robin. She felt sick.

"Blow on it," suggested April, peering over her shoulder.

Robin blew gently and bluish flames sprang up, licking one of the sticks. April passed her more crumpled-up paper, and Robin pushed it around the kindling. She kept blowing on the flames, and after a few minutes, the sticks crackled and snapped. She carefully rested three logs on top and closed the stove door. "We did it," she breathed.

Molly had climbed off the bed and was standing behind the girls. "I'm hungry," she whimpered. There were tear streaks on her face.

"We've got food," said April. "It's going to be just like having a picnic, Molly."

The wind whined like a wild animal outside the cabin, rattling the windows. Robin unpacked the sleeping bags from the bins under the bunks. The girls took off their boots. They each snuggled inside a bag and huddled on the floor close to the stove. Molly opened the bag of trail mix and took a huge handful.

"Don't take all the Smarties," warned Robin. She dug into the bag. As she munched, she tried to organize her thoughts. She wasn't ready to think about the horrible experience in the blizzard yet. It was still too real—the numbing cold, the pellets of snow stinging her face, her terror that Molly was lost somewhere. She slid a glance toward April. Her cousin had pulled her sleeping bag up to her chin and was picking at some trail mix.

Robin frowned. The fight with April seemed so long ago. One minute they had been having fun, cutting up magazines, and then she had found that stupid letter. She tested her feelings, trying to remember exactly

what April had told Stephanie. *The school is boring...*
Robin is acting weird. She sighed. None of it was fair,
but she didn't feel angry anymore. Just kind of tired.

Suddenly Dad's voice, full of static, filled the cabin.
"Girls, do you read me? Do you read me?"

"Dad!" screeched Molly.

Robin hopped to the table in her sleeping bag. Dad
always sounded like he was trying to contact Mars
when he spoke on the radio. She pushed the speaker
button. "Dad! It's us! We're fine!"

"All of you? Molly?"

"Molly too. We're fine," repeated Robin.

"Thank God." Robin could hear Dad take a big
breath. "What happened?"

Robin glanced at Molly. "It's a long story."

Dad quickly turned into Mom's clone. "Have you
got anything to eat? Have you managed to fire up the
stove?"

"We're toasty," said Robin proudly. She eyed the
woodbox. "We have enough wood to last all night.
And we've got power bars and trail mix."

"Do not...I repeat, DO NOT go outside. Do you
have any idea...almost thirty below..." Dad's voice
became buried in static.

"We won't," promised Robin.

Molly wriggled free of her sleeping bag. She danced at Robin's side. "I want to talk to Dad."

"I don't know if he can hear you." Robin held the button down and Molly shouted, "Daddy! It's me."

For a few seconds, Dad's voice was clear. "Molly, why do I think you're behind this? We'll talk at home."

More static and then snatches of Dad's voice.

"...snowmobile in the morning...NOT GO OUTSIDE...I repeat..."

Robin grinned. Even dads could freak out.

"See you tomorrow," she said. "Over and out."

The girls stripped off their jackets. Robin peered out the window at the darkening sky. It was hard to tell if it was still snowing. While April put another log in the stove, Robin lit the two oil lamps.

Molly filled the empty space between Robin and April with chatter. "Do you think I'm going to get in trouble? Should we play cards? I wish we had some hot chocolate."

"We do!" said Robin, jumping up. She had remembered the tin of hot-chocolate powder in the cupboard. She grabbed a pot and opened the door a crack to scoop up snow that had drifted up against the cabin wall. Then she set the pot on the stove.

It was amazing how much snow it took to make three cups of water. Each time Robin opened the door, a blast of frigid air swept inside, making Molly shriek with excitement.

They all agreed that it was the best hot chocolate they had ever had. Molly finished first. Full of huge yawns, she only protested a tiny bit when Robin tucked her into her sleeping bag in the bottom bunk. "I'm going to stay awake because I don't want to miss anything," she mumbled. Her eyes floated shut and her thumb drifted into her mouth.

April had found a deck of cards and was laying out a game of solitaire on the table. "There's another deck if you want to play double," she said.

"That's okay." Robin sat on a chair beside her. She sipped her hot chocolate and watched April flip cards for a few minutes. Suddenly April shoved all the cards across the table. "I'm going back," she said.

Robin froze. "What do you mean?"

April stared at her. "I phoned Stephanie this morning. She says I can live with her."

"But Mom and Dad—"

"Your dad knows. We discussed it. He has to talk to your mom, but he was pretty sure she'll understand. He said it might have been the wrong decision for me to come here in the first place."

"So it's not definite then." Robin stalled for time, trying to make sense of the feelings colliding inside her.

"It's definite enough. Your dad's on my side."

"And I'm not?"

April's cheeks flushed. "It doesn't feel like it," she muttered.

Robin opened her mouth to protest. Then she clamped her mouth shut tight. She didn't know what to say.

Silence.

Finally April said, "So are you mad again?"

"No," said Robin. Her hands were shaking. She put her mug of hot chocolate down and pressed her hands against her legs. She swallowed. "It was all my fault anyway. The accident and everything."

"What do you mean?" said April.

Robin's words came out in a rush. "I told Aunty Liz I would never ever forgive her if she didn't try. I begged her." She twirled the hot chocolate around the bottom of her mug. "I think that's why she did it," she finished miserably.

"That's not why," said April slowly. "It was because of me. I had a fit. I even cried when Mom said we might have to miss Christmas at the ranch. I said she was going to wreck everyone's Christmas. I acted worse than Molly ever does."

Both girls were silent for a moment. Robin's heart pounded. "Why do you talk to Molly about the accident but you don't talk to me?"

"Because she's interested," said April.

"So am I," said Robin.

"So then why do you change the subject every time it comes up?" said April. "You've never even asked me one question."

"I have," said Robin weakly.

"No, you haven't. You act like it never happened. Like everything is just supposed to be normal."

Robin swallowed. "I guess I didn't want you to get upset."

"Maybe I would get upset." April's voice shook. "But this is worse. It feels like you don't care."

"Then tell me. Please," said Robin.

April stared at Robin. She took a big breath. "I was so scared when we were driving. Mom wasn't saying anything. And I kept thinking I should tell her to go back. But I didn't. I've wished so many times that we could do that day over again."

"Me too," whispered Robin. "What happened? I mean, exactly, when the truck hit you."

"It was so fast. You couldn't see anything. Just white. And then suddenly there was this huge truck right in our face. I don't know after that. I remember hearing screaming. I think it must have been me. And then Mom kept saying, 'Everything's okay. Everything's okay.' And then there were flashing red lights and people, and I don't remember much after that."

Robin shuddered. What if it had been her family? "You must think about it all the time."

"I did at first," said April. "I was afraid to go to sleep in case I dreamed it all over again. It's a bit better now. Your mom's been really great to talk to."

Robin nodded. "Aunty Liz…her injuries?"

She listened quietly while April explained about pins and traction. "I have to be in Vancouver," she finished. "I have to be closer to Mom. It's got nothing to do with you. Do you get that?"

"I do," said Robin. And she *did*. It was what she would want too.

April grinned suddenly. "Best out of five for double solitaire. Come on, it's what we always do."

"Best out of ten," said Robin. "It's time we changed the rules."

Dad had said he would come for them in the morning on the snowmobile. That meant they had all night to talk and be together. She planned to make the most of it.

Chapter Twelve

"Done," said Robin in a satisfied voice. She stepped back and surveyed their project. Kim had come over after school, and she and Robin and April had started putting the castle together right away. It was perfect.

An ice castle. Stephanie had come up with the idea on the phone yesterday afternoon. She had read about it in a kids' magazine.

The castle was built from different sizes and shapes of blocks of ice. Mom had helped with that part last night when she got back from Vancouver, contributing ice-cream pails, a muffin tin, yogurt and margarine containers and an ice-cube tray. They had filled the containers with water and let them freeze overnight.

April had thought of putting red and blue and green food coloring in some of the containers. It gave the castle...*distinction*, Robin decided.

At first the blocks of ice kept falling over. Then Dad suggested mixing water and snow together to make slush to stick the blocks together. Dad's Marvelous Mortar, he called it. It had worked perfectly.

"I love it," declared Molly.

Kim frowned. "It needs something...Wait!" She clumped through the snow to the porch. She reached up and broke off a long icicle. "A spire!"

When the spire was carefully "glued" to the tower with Dad's mortar and three more were added (to give it balance, Dad said), the ice castle was declared finished.

"How are you going to get it to school?" said Molly.

"We're not," said Robin. "This is a practice. We'll make another one at school on Thursday."

"Will April be gone by then?"

"No. April has five more sleeps."

She was going to miss April, Robin knew that for sure. But in some ways, she was looking forward to life getting back to normal. Mom had brought back good reports from Vancouver about Aunty Liz and had assured both Robin and April that none of it was their fault. Her exact words had been, "Nonsense! My sister has always had a mind of her own, and she had made up her mind to come to the ranch for Christmas!"

Molly hopped around the castle. "Can I keep it?"

Robin looked at April and Kim. They nodded. "Sure. Until it melts," said Robin.

She hugged her arms to her chest. It was getting cold. The slush had soaked her mittens, and her fingers were freezing. Kim was staying for dinner, and then Robin planned to dive into a new book about training colts that her mother had brought back from Vancouver. She wanted to be ready in the spring for Kedar.

Maybe in the summer Stephanie and April could both come up to the ranch. They could ride the horses and—Robin grinned. She *liked* making plans.

Mom stuck her head out the kitchen door. "Anybody on the work crew need a hot-chocolate break?"

"Before *dinner*?" said Molly ecstatically.

"Ummm…why not?"

"Marshmallows?" said Molly.

"Don't push your luck," said Dad. "Mom is still Mom."

"Come on, Mol," said April. "Race you in!"

Robin lingered behind. Someone turned on the Christmas lights and their tiny reflections winked in the walls of the ice castle. She loved Christmas lights. Someone should invent spring lights and summer lights and fall lights.

The door opened. It was Molly. "Robin, everyone's going to play Madeline. *Madeline*! Hurry!"

Robin took one last look at the glittering castle. It was perfect for as long as it lasted.

Acknowledgments

I would like to thank my editor, Sarah Harvey, for her amazing attention to detail and her ability to get at the heart of my stories. I would also like to thank my sister, Janet, for her invaluable insight and suggestions.

Becky Citra is the author of more than a dozen books for young readers. She has written two popular series for Orca: the Ellie and Max historical novels and the Jeremy and the Enchanted Theater time-travel books. Becky lives on a ranch in Bridge Lake, British Columbia.